FOR A CHILD

By Rachel Field

Illustrations by
Elizabeth Orton Jones

This is a prayer written for one little girl, but it is a prayer for boys and girls all over the world. It is full of the intimate gentleness for familiar things, the love of friends and family, and the kindly protection of God. It carries a universal appeal for all ages and races, and brings to our hearts and minds the deep responsibility of preserving for all times the faith and hopes of little children.

PRAYER
FOR A CHILD

BY RACHEL FIELD
PICTURES BY ELIZABETH ORTON JONES

New York · THE MACMILLAN COMPANY · 1957

FOR HANNAH

PRAYER FOR A CHILD

Bless this milk and bless this bread.
Bless this soft and waiting bed
Where I presently shall be
Wrapped in sweet security.
Through the darkness, through the night
Let no danger come to fright
My sleep till morning once again
Beckons at the window pane.
Bless the toys whose shapes I know,
The shoes that take me to and fro
Up and down and everywhere.
Bless my little painted chair.
Bless the lamplight, bless the fire,
Bless the hands that never tire
In their loving care of me.
Bless my friends and family.
Bless my Father and my Mother
And keep us close to one another.
Bless other children, far and near,
And keep them safe and free from fear.
So let me sleep and let me wake
In peace and health, for Jesus' sake.
                         Amen.

less this milk and bless this bread.

Bless this soft and waiting bed
Where I presently shall be
Wrapped in sweet security

Through the darkness, through the night
Let no danger come to fright
My sleep till morning once again
Beckons at the window pane

less the toys whose shapes I know

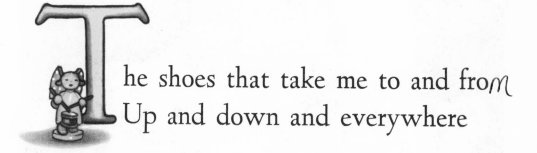

The shoes that take me to and from
Up and down and everywhere

less my little painted chair

less the lamplight, bless the fire

less the hands that never tire
In their loving care of me

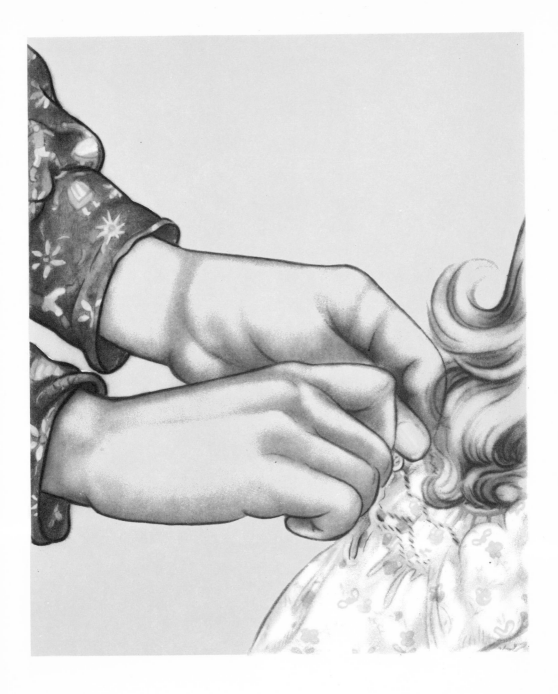

less my friends and family

less my Father and my Mother
And keep us close to one another

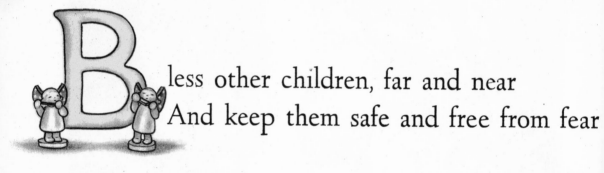

Bless other children, far and near
And keep them safe and free from fear

o let me sleep and let me wake
In peace and health, for Jesus' sake

Date Due

DEC 14 '65		OC 17 '84	OCT 17 '84
		NO 07 '84	OCT 22 '84
JAN 19 '66			
MAR 4 '66			
MAR 11 '66			
MAR 29 '66			
MAY 17 '66			
OCT 17 '66			
OCT 31 '66			
NOV 8 '66			
APR 10 '68	APR 17 '68		
MAY 22 '68	MAY 16 '68		
	1 3 '68		
JUL 10 '69	JUL 10 '69		
MAR 10 '71	MAR 9 '71		
NOV 7 '72	OCT 26 72		
DEC 6 '74	NOV 26 74		
NOV 5 '79	DEC 7 79		